MARVEL
GUARDIANS OF THE GALAXY

GAMORA'S GALACTIC SHOWDOWN

SUSTAINABLE
FORESTRY
INITIATIVE

Certified Sourcing

www.sfiprogram.org
SFI-01415

marvelkids.com

Designed by Kurt Hartman

STARRING

GAMORA

BY **BRANDON T. SNIDER**

ILLUSTRATED BY

PASCALE QUALANO

AND **CHRIS SOTOMAYOR**

Los Angeles
New York

FEATURING YOUR FAVORITES!

GAMORA

ROCKET

PIP THE TROLL

ADAM WARLOCK

NEBULA

THE COLLECTOR

THANOS

THE GODSLAY

THE CHITAURI

THE GEGKU

A MYSTERIOUS BOX

THE KODABAKS

A DEVIL CORKER

GROOT

DRAX

STAR-LORD

THE STORY OF GAMORA

*T*he Zen-Whoberis were a peaceful humanoid race, living in harmony, until a group of violent aliens arrived on their planet. The militaristic creatures invaded, destroying everything in their path and wiping the Zen-Whoberis completely off the cosmic map. When the dust settled, there was a single survivor, an infant known as **GAMORA**. The child was taken in by the mad

Titan **THANOS**, who sought to turn her into a war machine, molded precisely to do his evil bidding. He delighted in pitting Gamora against her adopted sister, **NEBULA**, and the two little girls fought for their father's affection. Gamora became an expert fighter and swordswoman, her viciousness earning her quite the bad reputation. But when she realized just how much she'd been manipulated by her villainous father, Gamora rebelled. She decided instead to become a force for good. Thanos was more than displeased, vowing ultimate revenge on Gamora for disobeying his orders. Nebula, however, stood by her father and shamed her sister for her disobedience. Gamora aligned herself with a handful of adventurers over the years until eventually settling down with the Guardians of the Galaxy.

Despite her alliances, she remains an outsider searching for kinship in a vast and unsettling universe, struggling to come to terms with her painful past. For the moment, she's content being known as *GAMORA: THE DEADLIEST WOMAN IN THE GALAXY.*

CHAPTER 1

A warm wind blew across the surface of **Degenera** as four Gegku hunters angrily marched through the planet's spaceship graveyard. They were looking for treasure. The large reptilian brutes lacked finesse in battle, relying on crude weaponry to do their dirty work. On this day, the Gegku came to Degenera equipped with firearms and prepared to challenge anyone that stood in their way.

"Search the area!" Wazzal, the leader,

commanded. **"Take everything you find and destroy the rest."** The Gegku stormed through the murky cemetery, tossing trash and scrap metal aside as if it were paper. Spaceships often got caught in Degenera's thick, polluted atmosphere, falling from the sky to be scavenged on the ground. The foul environment also made it the perfect place to hide. All of these things made Degenera a hub for criminal activity. But the planet wasn't all bad. There were small communities of harmless wanderers spread out across the surface. **"Wazzal, over here!"** the Gegku hunter shouted. **"I found something."** He used his rifle to poke at a large piece of metal. A tiny rodentlike creature scuttled out from under it. Wazzal grabbed it by the tail, dangling the terrified beastie back and forth as it tried to escape. **"HA-HA-HA! Look at this weak thing wiggle. How pathetic!"**

A pair of glowing white eyes opened amid the darkness.

GAMORA leaped from her hiding place into the middle of the Gegku hunters, sweeping her leg in a circle and knocking them off their feet. She unsheathed her sword and swiftly sliced the Gegku's weapons into pieces. The soldiers were paralyzed with fear. They'd never seen anyone move so fast.

Gamora turned her attention to Wazzal, grabbing his collar and pulling him close. "Wiggle for me, weak thing," she whispered in his ear, tossing the lizard man into a pool of bubbling ooze nearby. The hunters didn't dare say a word.

"Without your weapons, you're nothing but sad, ugly creatures," Gamora taunted. She looked down to see the sheepish alien critter Wazzal had frightened. It was staring at her. "You're safe now," she said. Then she turned to the Gegku. "But you're not."

She pressed a button on her wrist gauntlet

and a hologram appeared.

"Where is this item?" Gamora asked. "Tell me now."

"**Nuh-nuh-nuh . . .**" Wazzal stuttered nervously.

"Spit it out," Gamora challenged. She was losing patience quickly.

"**Nuh-nuh-never seen it before in my life,**" Wazzal said, his shaking body sinking into the goop. "**There's a place you might be able to find such a thing, but it's just a rumor.**"

"Where?" Gamora demanded.

"**Zaldrex,**" Wazzal replied, still trembling. "**I've heard the stories about you, Gamora. They said you were just like your father. Now I see the stories are—**"

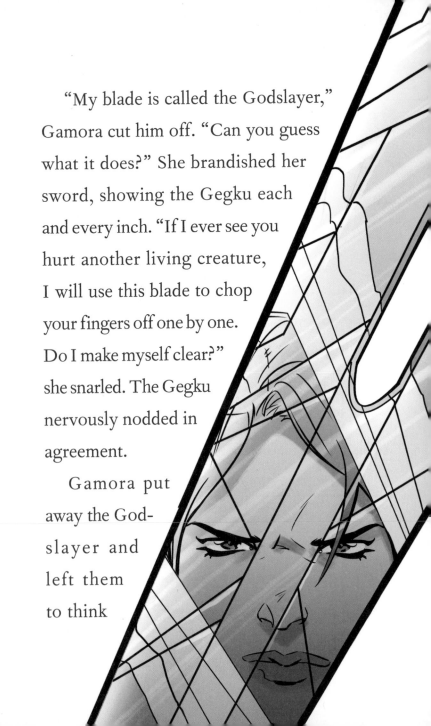

"My blade is called the Godslayer," Gamora cut him off. "Can you guess what it does?" She brandished her sword, showing the Gegku each and every inch. "If I ever see you hurt another living creature, I will use this blade to chop your fingers off one by one. Do I make myself clear?" she snarled. The Gegku nervously nodded in agreement.

Gamora put away the God- slayer and left them to think

deeply about what she had said. Chopping off fingers wasn't usually her style, but the threat always seemed to give her enemies a new perspective. Gamora spotted a small town in the distance and began walking toward it. She'd only been on **Degenera** a few days, but she was desperate to leave. *Where do I go next?* It had been a while since Gamora had seen her friends. She'd taken a leave of absence from the Guardians of the Galaxy when the universe presented her with an unexpected quest. Was she searching for a simple box, or was her mission much more than that?

Gamora found herself restless and wondered if she might also be searching for peace of mind.

After walking for what seemed like miles, Gamora came upon a dingy diner on the outskirts of a small community. She'd been traveling without a vehicle, hitching rides from transport vessels to get where she needed to go. Now it was time to find a new ride and leave Degenera for good. She watchfully entered the establishment, scanning every inch of it for danger. The air was thick, and smelled like smoke and meat. There were hordes of cantankerous alien creatures from across the universe, and all of them were giving Gamora the stink-eye. They all knew her reputation. Finding a ride wasn't going to be easy.

"I need a way off this planet," Gamora said to the alien cook in the grease-soaked apron. He silently pointed to someone in the corner. When Gamora turned to see who, she was surprised by a familiar face.

"Well, well, well," said Rocket, spinning himself around in his chair. **"Hitching rides? C'mon, Gamora. You know better than that."**

Despite her desire for solitude, Gamora was happy to see a friend. Even though he was cranky most of the time, **Rocket** had a good heart and a warrior's spirit.

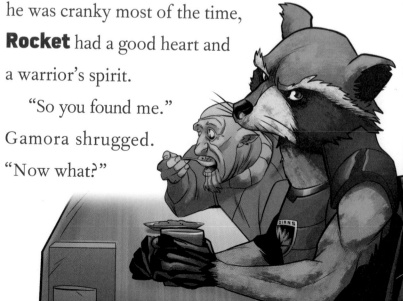

"So you found me." Gamora shrugged. "Now what?"

"**Why don't you end your vacation and come back to the Guardians? No questions asked,**" Rocket continued. "**Things aren't the same without you. Drax can't stop crying! And you don't want to know what Groot won't stop doing.**"

Gamora was flattered but in no mood for jokes. "I'm better off alone," she said, looking away, embarrassed.

Just then a group of renegade **Kodabaks** burst into the diner. The Kodabaks were surly piglike creatures who served many evil masters.

"**You're sitting in my seat, animal,**" griped the alien hog, tapping Rocket on the shoulder. The Kodabak's breath was hot, and it stank like sewage.

"**Until you do something about that swamp breath, I'm not moving!**" Rocket said. "**This is a free planet, and I can sit anywhere I want. Got that?**"

Five more Kodabaks closed in on Rocket, and things got serious.

"Okay, okay," he said, rising from his chair. **"So maybe it is your seat, after all."**

Gamora's body tensed. "Stay seated," she said, pushing Rocket back down.

The Kodabak leader rudely looked Gamora up and down. **"You're pretty,"** he began. **"For a green-skin."** He and his swinish friends let out a hearty chuckle, and Gamora flew into action. She gently slid her foot under the table nearby, flipping it up into the air to land safely in her hands. She flung it at the cackling Kodabaks, knocking them down with a **_THUD_**. The diner erupted into total chaos.

"RUN!" Rocket shouted, grabbing Gamora by the arm and pulling her out the door.

"I hope we're running toward a ship," Gamora replied.

"Don't you worry. Good ol' Rocket has you covered," he said, sprinting down a long alleyway and through an encampment. They darted over and around fruit sellers, trinket peddlers, and the occasional pile of animal droppings. Soon the Kodabaks were gaining on them. Gamora spotted a tower of empty barrels and toppled them over to trip up the pudgy hog-men. It only bought them a few moments.

"Almost there!" said Rocket, rounding the corner. He wasn't prepared for what happened next. **"WHAT THE KRUTAK?!"** he shouted. **"My ship is gone!"**

CHAPTER 2

*G*amora was frustrated. She'd been lying low and minding her own business, but now she was on the run from a bunch of angry pig-men with Rocket Raccoon in tow. It wasn't at all what she'd planned for or expected. The ship that was supposed to save them was missing, and they only had moments to figure out what to do next.

"D'AST!" exclaimed Rocket, taking off in another direction. **"This way!"**

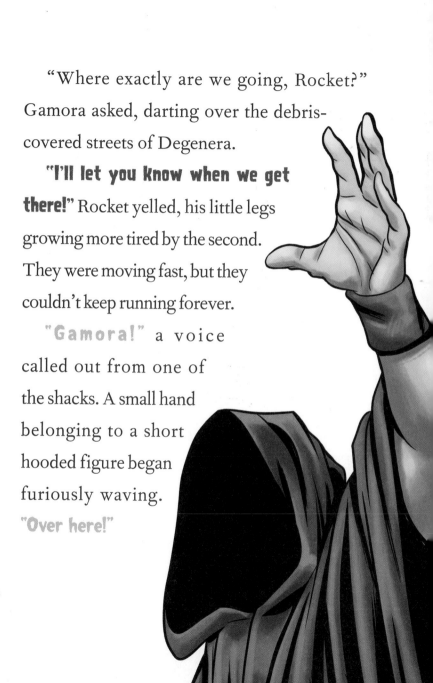

"Where exactly are we going, Rocket?" Gamora asked, darting over the debris-covered streets of Degenera.

"I'll let you know when we get there!" Rocket yelled, his little legs growing more tired by the second. They were moving fast, but they couldn't keep running forever.

"Gamora!" a voice called out from one of the shacks. A small hand belonging to a short hooded figure began furiously waving. **"Over here!"**

Rocket looked at Gamora wide-eyed. **"You got friends here you didn't tell me about?"** he asked, sweaty and wheezing. They rushed into the shabby living quarters as the Kodabaks ran by without a glance. Rocket and Gamora breathed a sigh of relief, having escaped their enemies. The shack was damp and smelled of body odor. Its owner slowly removed his hood, revealing a familiar face.

"Welcome to Degenera," said **Pip the Troll**. "Sorry about the smell." Pip had known Gamora for many years. They were once members of the Infinity Watch, a handful of heroes who traveled the galaxy looking for the fabled Infinity Stones. It was a difficult task

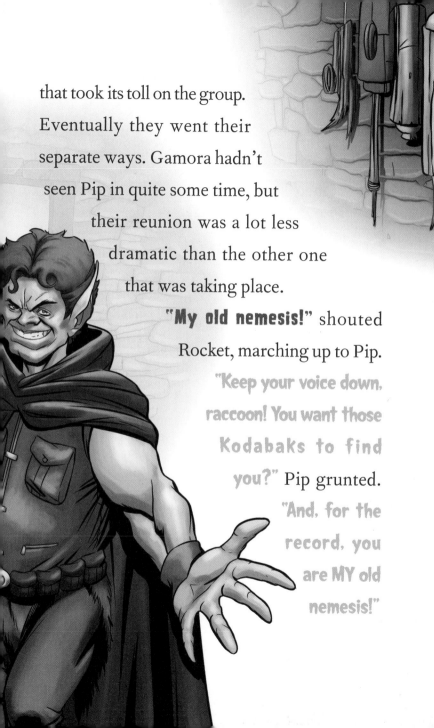

that took its toll on the group. Eventually they went their separate ways. Gamora hadn't seen Pip in quite some time, but their reunion was a lot less dramatic than the other one that was taking place.

"My old nemesis!" shouted Rocket, marching up to Pip.

"Keep your voice down, raccoon! You want those Kodabaks to find you?" Pip grunted. "And, for the record, you are MY old nemesis!"

Pip and Rocket had crossed paths before, many years ago, before either one of them had ever met Gamora. It hadn't gone well.

"I'm not a raccoon, and you know that! YOU KNOW THAT!" Rocket said in a heated whisper.

"Hello, Pip," Gamora said, eyeing the cramped space. "It's good to see you, even under these strange circumstances."

"It's weird, all right. But good!" Pip said warmly. **"The universe is a small place, I guess."**

"I didn't know you and Rocket had history," Gamora said. "Will working together be a problem?"

"HA!" cackled Rocket. **"No. I'm a professional.**

I'm here to help you. That's what friends are for, right?"

"Yeah, me too," added Pip. "Whatever you need, I'm there for you. That's what friends are for."

"**I JUST SAID**—" Rocket closed his eyes and took a very deep breath. "**Keep it together, Rocket. You're better than this.**"

"What brings you to Degenera?" asked Pip. "It's not exactly paradise."

"I'm searching for an item," Gamora said, activating her holographic projector. "A box that once belonged to my father, **Thanos**." Rocket and Pip shuddered. Thanos was one of the galaxy's most notorious villains, after all.

Being Gamora's father didn't make him any less scary.

"What's inside that thing?" Rocket asked.

Gamora paused. "I don't know," she confessed. "I was told never to touch it. When I was a girl, I always believed it contained something of value to my father, something powerful. He used it as a bargaining chip to gain my obedience. Once, I caught my sister trying to open it, but she was unable to do so. When I grabbed it, snatching the box from her grasp, it began to open. I believe I know why, but before either of us could see inside, Thanos angrily swiped it from my hands. I never saw it again, but I remember what it looks like, every single inch. I know Nebula does as well. It could all be a mind game of my father's design, or it could be . . . something else."

"OooOooOoo, you mean like an Infinity Stone?" asked Pip.

"As a girl I dreamed that whatever was in that box could take me far away. Away from the madness . . . It's silly to think about now," Gamora confided. "It fell out of Thanos's hands and went missing. For years I've been following rumors and reports of its whereabouts, as if it were a strange myth. Leads always seemed to run dry, and I eventually gave up looking. That's when it reappeared. I received an image from a cosmic trading post that confirmed the box's existence in the region. It's changing hands quickly and I need to find it immediately."

"So what are we waiting for? Let's go find

this thing so you can come on home to the Guardians of the Galaxy. Your real team," Rocket said, shaking his finger at Pip. "This troll will teleport us anywhere we need to go. It's the only thing he's good for!"

"Um, well, uh, I've got some bad news," Pip said sheepishly. "My teleporting powers have been kind of nutty lately."

"Oh, great. The troll is broken! He's useless!" Rocket said, pacing around the tiny hut in a fervor. "What do we do now? Fly a holo-banner across the Milky Way?"

TWO AMAZING HEROES AND A TROLL SEEK MYSTERY BOX ONCE OWNED BY AN EVIL, ALL-POWERFUL TITAN.

"I can still track stuff, you mangy beast!" Pip said, sticking his finger in Rocket's face.

"**STOP**. Both of you. There's more," Gamora began. "My sources have told me that my sister, **Nebula**, has also been tracking the box. Although neither of us can confirm its contents, I fear that if that box falls into her hands, the entire universe could be in danger."

"**So, troll, how do we get off this stinky planet? Some flarknard stole my rental ship,**" Rocket grumped.

"I'm glad you asked." Pip said, opening a curtain to reveal a small old spacecraft.

"**You want the three of us to fly around in that fossilized hunk of junk?**" asked Rocket. "**I've seen bathrooms bigger than this! You're out of your mind, stubby.**"

"I like to think of it as vintage cozy," Pip said, patting the spaceship's side. A metal panel fell off, exposing its ancient circuitry. "Heh-heh. Nothing to see here."

Gamora rolled her eyes and wondered whether involving Rocket and Pip in her quest was the right choice. But there was no time to think about it. They all climbed into the cramped vessel and prepared for takeoff. Pip moved toward the main cabin and was brushed aside by Rocket.

"Beat it, troll. I'm flyin' this thing," Rocket said, sitting down in the captain's chair.

"Talk to me like that again, raccoon. See what happens," Pip countered.

"I. AM. NOT. A. RACCOON," Rocket said, his voice rising.

"That hairy mug of yours has 'raccoon' written all over it," Pip scoffed.

"Why don't you try putting a mask on, tiny? I'm sick of looking at that ugly troll face," Rocket barked.

"Say it one more time, Raccoon!" Pip growled.

"ENOUGH!" Gamora boomed. She was

getting a headache. "Listen to these words, as I'll only say them once: settle your differences."

"**Fine**," said Rocket, surrendering his chair. "**I'm going to go put my feet up and try to forget that I let a stumpy little troll tell me what to do.**"

Pip settled into the captain's chair and began flipping switches. "**Strap in!**" he said, turning to Gamora. "**Where we headed?**"

"**Zaldrex,**" she said.

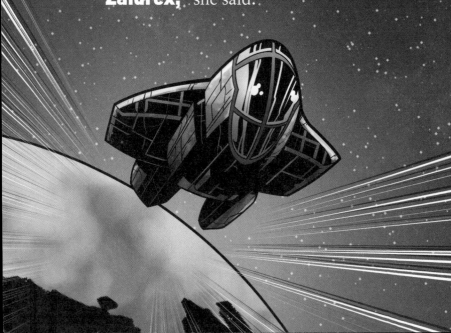

CHAPTER 3

ZZZGRUGGLEZZZZGRUGGLEZZ

A rumbling snore shook the inside of the tiny metal spacecraft.

"Is that Rocket?!" asked Pip, shaking his head in disbelief. "He sounds like a Varlaxican sludge beast."

Gamora stared out the window, distracted.

"You look good, kid. Been too long since we've caught up," Pip said, noticing Gamora's uneasiness. "Whatever you're thinking about,

don't let it get to you. We'll grab this box, and you'll be on your way in no time." He flipped a switch on the control panel, lighting up the monitors in front of them. Alien beings from a hundred worlds filled the screens.

"This is Zaldrex. On the outside it seems like some no-name planet," Pip explained. "But it's much more than that. You just have to go underground. The Collector runs a top secret thieves' market and auction house in the caverns underneath the planet's surface. He's got all kinds of nasty stuff down there, mostly the junk he doesn't want. I'm betting that's where you'll find what you're looking for. We'll disguise ourselves as riffraff and sneak in. I've got some counterfeit credits we can use to bid on it. They look just like the real thing! No one will ever know the difference."

Gamora stared intently at the screen. "Nebula will be there," she muttered. "I can feel it."

"**BLAHG!**" shouted Rocket, waking from his nap and rubbing his eyes. "**I had the worst nightmare. I was stuck on a spaceship with this chubby little troll, and . . .**" He sputtered, spotting Pip in the captain's chair. "**UGH! My nightmare came true!**"

"I don't know how you stand that guy,"
Pip said to Gamora, pulling back on the ship's
throttle. "Prepare for landing. We're here."

Pip brought the spaceship down on the
outskirts of Zaldrex's capital city. Then the trio
donned dark cloaks to disguise themselves. If
anyone recognized them, it would ruin the entire
plan. Following a winding staircase, they
traveled down into the thieves'
market casually and discreetly.
The market had many alien curi-
osities, all of which were deadly.
There were things like canisters of
disease and various cruel weapons
for sale. These were things meant to
inflict pain and suffering on countless
people. It made Gamora angry. Soon

she spotted something even worse: a tiny cage containing three alien children. The cage was being guarded by the Collector's thugs, a collection of the galaxy's worst bullies. While the guards were distracted, Gamora took a small bag of rations from inside her cloak and gave it to the children. The tasty treats brought a smile to their faces, and they eagerly scarfed them down as quickly as they could.

How could someone do this? Gamora thought.
It boiled her blood to see children separated
from their families, kept in cages, and waiting
to be sold like slaves. Her body tensed as she
considered ways to free them. But suddenly,
a siren sounded and an announcement blared
from the speakers above.

"THE AUCTION WILL NOW COMMENCE IN THE MAIN AREA!"

"This area is off-limits. Get moving!" one of the Collector's goons shouted, rudely pushing Gamora with the end of his rifle. It took everything she had not to grab his weapon and teach him a lesson, but there was a bigger plan in motion.

Before she left, Gamora spoke to the children in a whisper. "I will return, I promise," she said, placing her hand on the bars. "Do not be afraid." Still angry, she joined Pip and Rocket in the main hall, where the auction was getting under way.

"Welcome, brutes, devils, fiends, and beasts!" a voice echoed through the bustling chamber.

"I am Taneleer Tivan, known to you miscreants as the Collector. This evening I bring to you some of the rarest rubbish in the entire galaxy. One warlord's trash is another warlord's treasure, after all. Settle in, you'll not want to miss out."

"I'm ready," Pip said, holding his bidding paddle tightly.

The Collector had assembled an impressive amount of antiquities over the years, but often found himself with broken or worthless items. Instead of discarding these things, he decided to sell them. He knew his followers were too naïve to know none of the items had any real value. They bid with their hopes and dreams. The Collector brought forth numerous salvaged goods, some of which he'd only

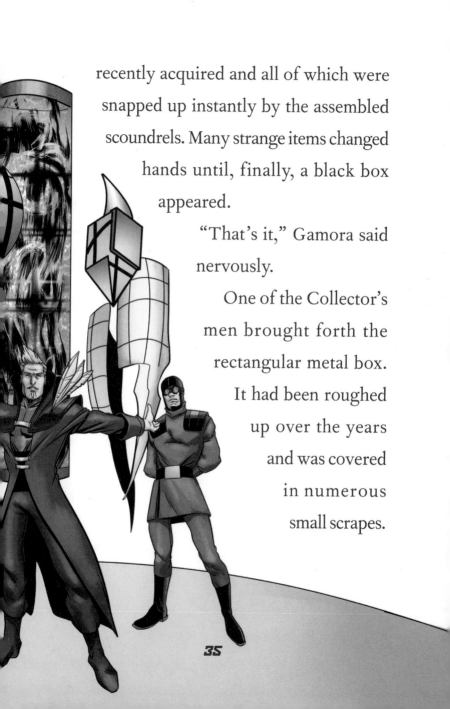

recently acquired and all of which were snapped up instantly by the assembled scoundrels. Many strange items changed hands until, finally, a black box appeared.

"That's it," Gamora said nervously.

One of the Collector's men brought forth the rectangular metal box. It had been roughed up over the years and was covered in numerous small scrapes.

The crowd seemed uninterested. No one knew it once belonged to the mighty Thanos. The Collector stared at it for a moment. He'd never seen it before. His associate leaned in and whispered the details of its retrieval in his ear.

"Ah, yes. This was recovered from a space trawler near Titan. Shall we see what's inside?" teased the Collector, attempting to pry open the lid. The task was giving him some difficulty, and he was not pleased. "Cosmic junk. Who wants it? Bidding begins at one hundred credits!"

"What do I do?" asked Pip, flustered.

"Raise your paddle and bid on it, troll!" Rocket said in a loud whisper.

Pip raised his bidding paddle. The Collector immediately nodded in confirmation.

"Going once...going twice..." The Collector paused, looking around the room. **"Sold to the troll in the hood! Pay your one hundred credits and come get this sad piece of trash."** As Pip made his way forward, a familiar blue-skinned figure bounded through the audience, landing squarely onstage. It was Nebula. She snatched the box out of the Collector's hands and took off in another direction, laughing wildly. The Collector was quite displeased. **"Get her and get that ugly box!"** he shouted. But before his minions began their chase, a distraction arose in the audience. Rocket was voicing his agitation.

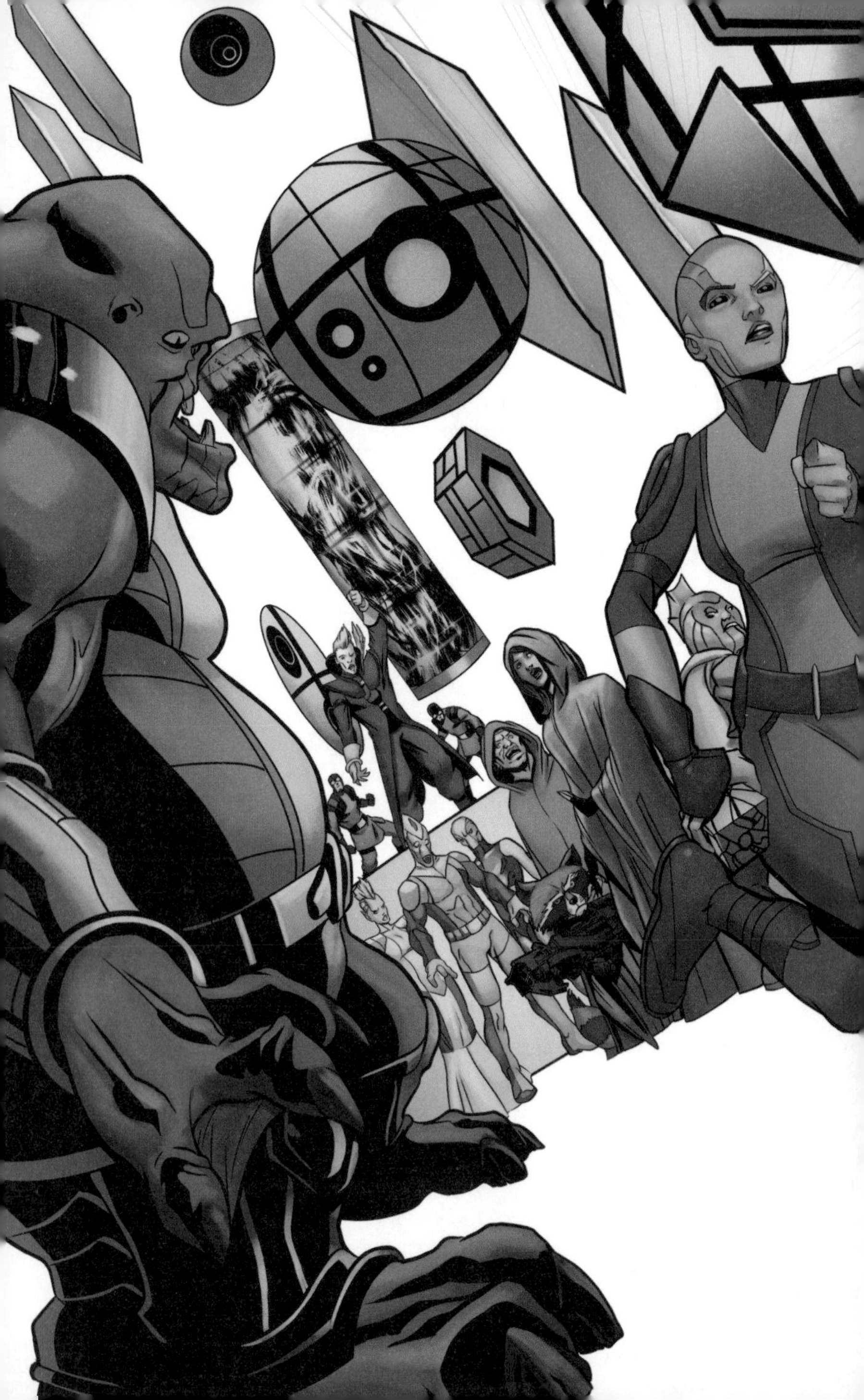

"Un-krutakin'-believable!" Rocket shouted, whipping off his cloak in anger and revealing his plasma cannon. It wasn't the wisest move. The Collector's eyes widened. Rocket had stolen from him in the past. Now was the time to make sure he paid the price.

"Get that animal!" screeched the Collector. As his crew of snarling bodyguards made their way toward Rocket, Gamora swung her leg out into the aisle, tripping them so that they fell like dominoes on top of one another.

"Time to go," Gamora said, pushing Rocket and Pip toward the exit. They took off after Nebula, but the Collector's goon squad was on their tail soon enough, chasing them wildly through the thieves' market. Laser beams nipped at Rocket's heels as he, Gamora, and

Pip rushed to their spaceship.

"D'AST! Watch it with the lasers, flarknard!" Rocket said, charging up his plasma cannon. **"You don't know who you're messing with!"**

"No, Rocket," Gamora commanded. "Get in the ship and be ready to take off. There's something I must do first."

Rocket grumbled to himself, pushing Pip up the ship's staircase. **"You heard the lady. In you go, troll! Let's get this garbage plane moving."**

Gamora darted back across the bazaar, throwing her hunters for a loop and losing them momentarily. At last she found the imprisoned alien children she'd encountered earlier. Gamora ripped open the door to their cage and freed them. "Are your parents safe?" she asked as they nodded in unison. "Go to them." The

little ones scurried away to safety and Gamora made a silent vow. **She'd one day return to Zaldrex and end the criminal activity that plagued it once and for all.** Hearing footsteps furiously approach, she then took off toward the spaceship.

CHAPTER 4

*T*he Collector's goons surrounded the spacecraft as Gamora stood defiantly before them. They thought they were more powerful than she was simply because they had weapons, but Gamora knew better. She looked at the assembled hooligans and wondered whether she should go easy on them. As they opened fire, Gamora drew her Godslayer blade and deflected each laser blast with ease. The fearless act left the Collector's thugs speechless. She used their amazement to her advantage. Grabbing their leader by the arms, she swung him like a rag doll, knocking his cohorts out cold. She bent down near the broken bully and left him with a message.

"You got off easy this time. I'm going to return to **Zaldrex** very soon—and, make no mistake, I will finish what I've started," she threatened. She took a final look around, boarded the ship, and took off into the stratosphere. As Rocket panted in the corner, Gamora stared out the window, thinking about the cruelty she'd seen in the thieves' market.

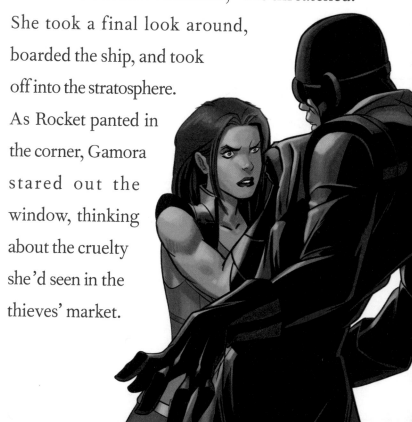

It gnawed at her so much, she forgot that their mission had been a failure.

"I'm sorry," Pip said, collapsing into the pilot's seat. "I wasn't fast enough to grab the box. I should have done something!"

"This wasn't your fault. Nebula always appears when you least expect her," Gamora said comfortingly. The group became silent and reflective.

BEEP! BEEP! BEEP! BEEP! BEEP!

"Someone is trying to hail us," Pip said, flipping a series of switches on the control panel. "The frequency's source is cloaked. I don't know who it is. Should I let the signal through?"

Gamora nodded affirmatively as Pip pressed a series of buttons. Nebula's face appeared on the screen before them.

"Hello, **Gamora**," growled Nebula. "When are you coming home? Father and I miss you." She held up the metal box she'd just stolen, inspecting every inch. "Do you like it? I don't know what could possibly be inside this plain old thing, but it must be something important if you're chasing after it."

"That doesn't belong to you," Gamora snapped.

"As long as my body is drawing breath, I'll

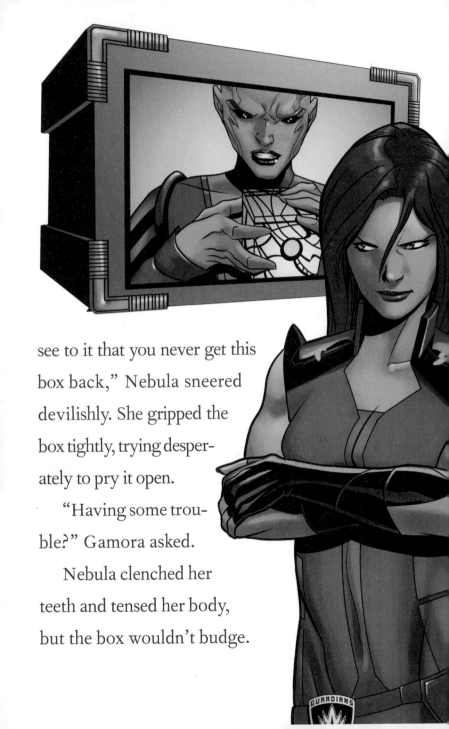

see to it that you never get this box back," Nebula sneered devilishly. She gripped the box tightly, trying desperately to pry it open.

"Having some trouble?" Gamora asked.

Nebula clenched her teeth and tensed her body, but the box wouldn't budge.

"Only I can open it," revealed Gamora. "Don't you recall what happened when we were children? I had my suspicions and now they've been confirmed. Only my touch can activate the mechanism. The box is worthless without me."

Nebula noticed the small fingerprint lock on the outside of the box and became infuriated. Her frenzied scream filled the ship's cabin before she disappeared from the monitors completely.

Rocket found her reaction endlessly amusing. **"HA-HA-HA!"** he cackled. **"Did you see her face?! Ol' Nebby did NOT like hearing that news. So what do we do now?"**

"Nebula knows we'll come for her. She'll be waiting for us," Gamora responded. "Patch me through to Carol Danvers. I need to talk to **Captain Marvel**."

"You got it! I'll just track her down using her Avengers comm link and then hack into whatever camera is nearby so we can see her beautiful smile," Pip said, pressing buttons and flipping switches on the old console. "This computer might be rickety, but I found her! She's busting up some trouble on the planet Ba-Banis. Patching her through now." Captain Marvel soon appeared on-screen. She had a Ba-Bani warrior in a headlock.

"**Smile, Cap!**" Rocket said, waving. "**And look up.**" Captain Marvel turned, squinting up at the nearby security camera.

"Rocket? I'm kind of busy at the moment," Carol said, squeezing the squirming Ba-Bani tighter. "Wait a second. Gamora, is that you?"

"Hi, Carol. I could use your help with something," Gamora began. She rarely asked for assistance, but Captain Marvel was a good friend and a powerful ally.

"I'd love to lend you a hand, but I'm pretty tied up with Avengers business at the moment. You know how it is with alien invasions. I'm definitely in for the next round of butt-kicking, though. Anything for family. Oh, and tell Star-Lord he owes me a mixtape!" Carol said. "**Captain Marvel OUT.**"

"I'll call the Guardians," Rocket said. "I think Quill and Groot are running errands on Spartax, but Drax should be around. He won't mind busting a few heads with us." Rocket pushed into Pip's space to enter a series of numbers on the keyboard. "This old technology is killing me!"

VIIIIIZZZZZZT!

The lights flickered inside the ship as the communication console sent sparks flying onto Pip's hairy troll feet.

"What happened?" Gamora asked.

"The power is going out, and we lost contact. But I can fix this!" Pip said, pressing buttons seemingly at random. Unexpectedly, the lights went out, leaving the ship in complete darkness.

"I knew we couldn't trust a troll," Rocket huffed, flipping on his flashlight.

"We have just enough power to make it to Morag IV," Pip said, changing course. "Pray we make it there in one piece."

CHAPTER 5

"Here we are. Morag IV," Pip sighed. He carefully brought the weakened spacecraft down through a small hole in the roof of an old abandoned temple. "It's about the best we can do until I figure out how to recharge this thing."

"You mean until *I* figure out how to recharge this thing," Rocket piped up, pointing his finger in Pip's face.

"Get that hairy digit out of my mug!" Pip countered. "Everyone listen up, because the climate on this planet is harsh. It's cold, dark, and dusty. Stay indoors!" Pip glanced at the back of the ship. The door was open, and Gamora was guardedly making her way through the darkened sanctuary. She wanted to find danger before it found her.

"Hello, old friends," a familiar voice echoed. Gamora recognized it immediately and was comforted. The empty chamber came alive in a burst of light, illuminating the detailed alien design covering the walls. **Adam Warlock** emerged from behind a giant column and greeted his guests. **"Welcome,"** he said warmly. **"What brings you around? I assume it's something Pip is to blame for, correct?"**

"YES!" Rocket said, marching up to Warlock and shaking his hand. **"Thanks for the temporary parking space, Adam."**

Adam Warlock was also once a member of the Infinity Watch. Not only was he a master at manipulating cosmic energies, he was also quite good at helping his friends achieve emotional balance. Gamora greeted him with a hug.

"It's been too long, Adam Warlock," she said, squeezing him tightly.

"Alone on some crusty old planet?" asked Pip. **"It's not exactly the coolest place for a cosmic legend. But it's still good to see an old pal."**

"I needed time away to figure some things out. And I sense I'm not the only one here who's felt that way of late," Warlock said, staring at Gamora. "Let's talk." Adam Warlock began walking down one of the long corridors, knowing Gamora would follow.

"Oh, sure, she gets the grand tour, and I'm stuck here with tiny," Rocket complained.

"You two go catch up," Pip said, shooing Gamora and Warlock away. "Don't worry about us. We'll get the ship working even if I have to make Raccoon Boy push it into orbit by hand!"

Gamora and Adam Warlock casually strolled through the cavernous temple, recalling old stories and making small talk. Warlock's presence comforted Gamora, but he could tell that something much more serious was on her mind. "What are

you looking for?" he asked abruptly.

Gamora took a long, deep breath. "A box," she began. "It belonged to my father."

Warlock let out a small chuckle. "No, no. What you're looking for is something much bigger and more important than a box. Thanos's dark shadow looms over so much of your life that you cannot find harmony."

Thanos. Her evil father's name stung Gamora's ears every time she heard it. She wondered whether Warlock was right. At first she had believed her quest was simply about a family heirloom, but it was clearly becoming about much more than that.

"Thanos made me who I am. No matter what I do in my life, I'm forever linked to his destructive legacy," Gamora confided, shaking her head in disbelief. "Maybe I'm looking for this box because I think it will help bring me a sense of peace. I don't seem to know anymore."

"You aren't defined by your father's evil deeds, Gamora. He manipulated you at a young age. You didn't understand what was happening, but you do now. In order to move forward, you must heal yourself," Adam continued. "The past can be difficult to deal with, especially when it's painful, but you can get through this. You're not alone. Myself, Pip, the Guardians—we're your friends.

We're your tribe. Let us help you." The duo had circled back around to the main chamber, and they heard Rocket and Pip arguing inside the spaceship. It made Gamora smile.

Adam Warlock's eyes began to glow. His body pulsed with the cosmic energies of a thousand worlds as he began weaving light into a solid form. Soon he produced a bizarre creation.

"This is a healing cocoon. It will allow you to rest; when you emerge again, you'll feel renewed and cleansed of negative energy," Adam explained.

Gamora looked over the incredible cocoon. She was mesmerized by the strange creation before her eyes. This is my chance to free myself, she

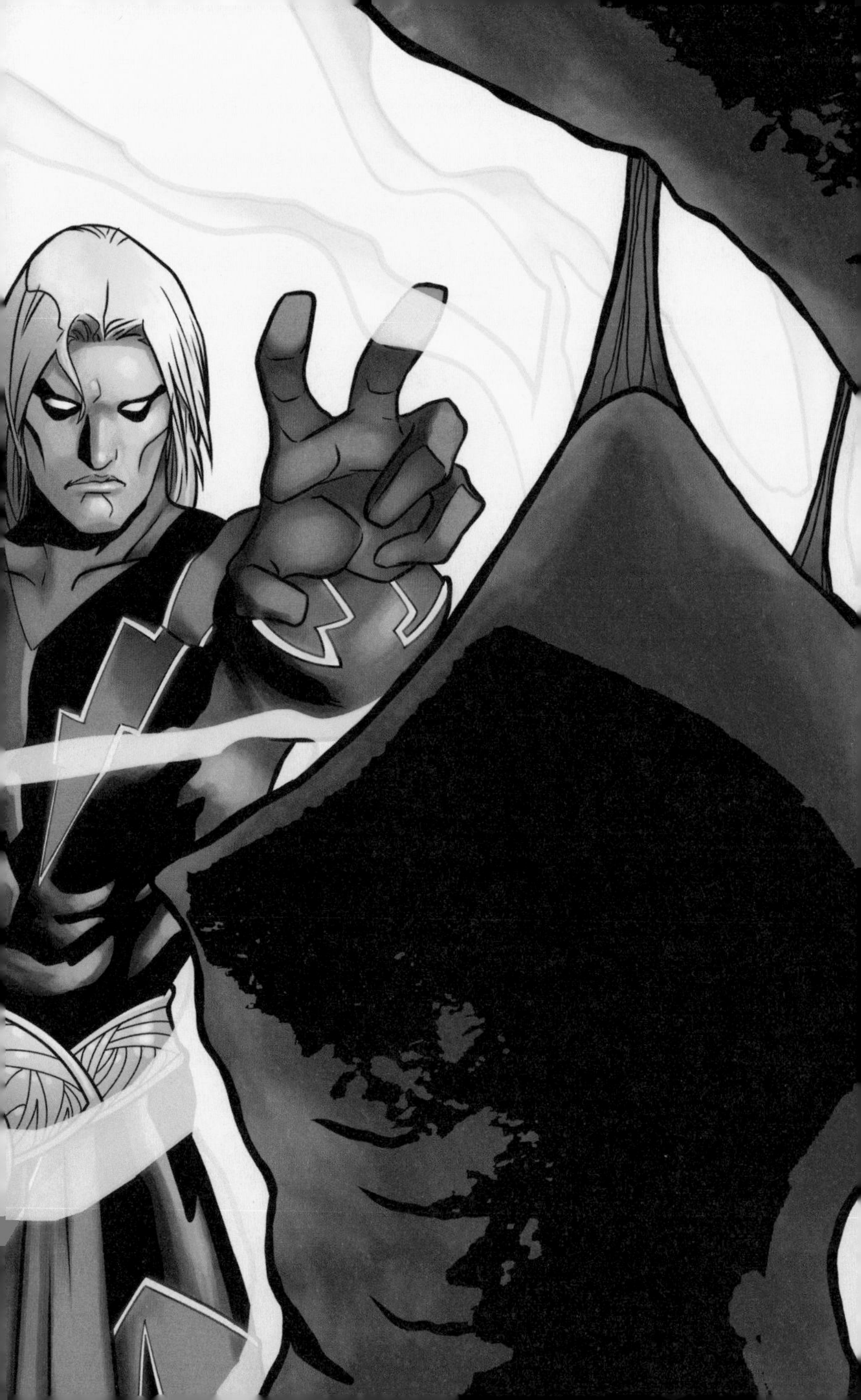

thought. But her natural instincts said something quite different. "If I'm immobilized, it will put you all at risk," she said.

"The process won't take long," Warlock assured her. **"We're on a desolate planet in the middle of nowhere. We'll be fine. Just remember: You are who you wish to be. Don't be frightened."**

Gamora found Warlock's optimism impressive. She cautiously stepped into the cocoon and lay down, clutching the hilt of her blade tightly against her chest. "Just in case," she whispered. In a swirl of radiance, Warlock used his powers to seal the cocoon, leaving Gamora to her rest. Rocket and Pip peeked their heads out of the spaceship to survey the strange creation.

"Weird," said Rocket.

"That's Adam Warlock for you," Pip responded.

Inside the cocoon, Gamora
had entered a dream state. She
awoke on a beautiful lush island.
Colorful creatures roamed nearby as the
gentle sound of a waterfall filled the air. She felt
the warm sun on her face, and it made her feel
blissful. Gamora was in paradise. A small bird
landed in front of her. As she knelt down for a
closer look, a giant boot came out of nowhere and
violently stomped on the bird. The skies grew
dark and stormy. Thanos had arrived.

Gamora was surprised by her father's

appearance, and backed away. As the stone-faced villain made his way toward her, the beautiful surroundings began to wither and die. The thriving flora and fauna soon transformed into a cold, barren desert. The relaxing waterfall was replaced by a sharp cliff leading down into a dark cavern. Gamora's peaceful feeling soon turned to rage.

"My unworthy disgrace of a daughter," Thanos began. **"You never thanked me for rescuing you from a life of weakness and defeat. I gave you power beyond your wildest imagination, training you to be a fierce warrior. Now you embarrass yourself by associating with a group of foolish space rangers. You were to be my ultimate weapon of destruction, and you threw it all away!"** Thanos stomped his boot, shaking the ground.

"I am no one's weapon!" Gamora shouted, moving into a defensive stance. "For so long I've felt shame over the abuse I suffered at your hands. You made me into a thing to be used only for violence. I was just a child." She unsheathed her blade. "It's time to settle our differences. You see, those space rangers are my best friends. They deserve your respect. And if you won't give it to me, I suppose I'll just have to take it."

"You are an animal, Gamora—obedient and submissive," Thanos growled. **"That is what you were trained to be."**

"I am a warrior. I use the skills I've learned to defend innocents from the likes of you!" Gamora explained. She lunged at Thanos with the Godslayer and the battle began.

In the real world outside the cocoon, Pip and Rocket struggled with the spaceship's ancient battery. Things weren't going well.

WATHOOM!!!

Suddenly, an enormous warship touched down, just outside Adam Warlock's sanctuary. The Collector's goons had arrived.

CHAPTER 6

"Adam Warlock!" the soldier bellowed. "Hand over the fugitives or prepare for combat." The Collector's thugs surrounded the temple, preparing to strike. Time was running out.

"Wake up Gamora," Rocket commanded. **"We need her NOW!"**

"No," Adam Warlock said firmly, glancing at the nearby cocoon. **"She must have her time to heal. We will have to handle this situation ourselves."**

Inside the cocoon, a fierce battle raged
between father and daughter.

CLANG! CLANG! CLANG!

The sound of Gamora's blade vibrated through
the air as it hit Thanos's gauntlets with blinding fury. He blocked her attacks with
ease, but Gamora remained unstoppable.
She was a master at physical combat
and wasn't about to give up. Thanos,
however, preferred mental warfare.
He enjoyed getting into his
enemies' heads and
using their
insecurities

against them, even when that enemy was his own daughter. **"What's in the mystery box, I wonder?"** he asked. **"Does it contain the most powerful item in the universe, or is it empty? Will your mission be worth it in the end, or will you have risked the lives of yourself and your friends for nothing?"**

These were questions Gamora had asked herself but was afraid to answer. What she knew for sure was that getting that box back was only part of her plan. The other part was dealing with her father's legacy of evil. It was time to finish Thanos. Gamora swung her sword around again, but this time Thanos caught it with his bare hands.

"Do you think that what's inside that box will tell you who you are?" Thanos taunted, tossing the Godslayer off a nearby cliff. Gamora could hear her treasured weapon bounce across the rocks as it fell. "Silly girl."

Fuming, Gamora grabbed Thanos by the arm and whipped him over her shoulder and onto the ground. She held him there, pinned, using every bit of strength she had, her body trembling from exhaustion. "I already know who I am!" she roared into her father's face.

Thanos was entertained. He threw off his daughter and stood, cackling wildly. "HA-HA-HA! You are everything I wanted you to be. You're a cruel warrior. This is what I made you. You'll never escape your heritage, Gamora. You are the daughter of THANOS!"

Gamora lunged at her father, striking him square in the gut. He smiled and she struck him again but this time even harder. That's what he'd trained her to do, after all. *Never yield*, he'd scream during her childhood training sessions. She heard her father's voice echo in her head and it filled her with fury. It no longer mattered that she was tired; she had a job to do. She continued to strike him, over and over again, until he became weary and unsteady. A rumbling tremor shook the ground, and

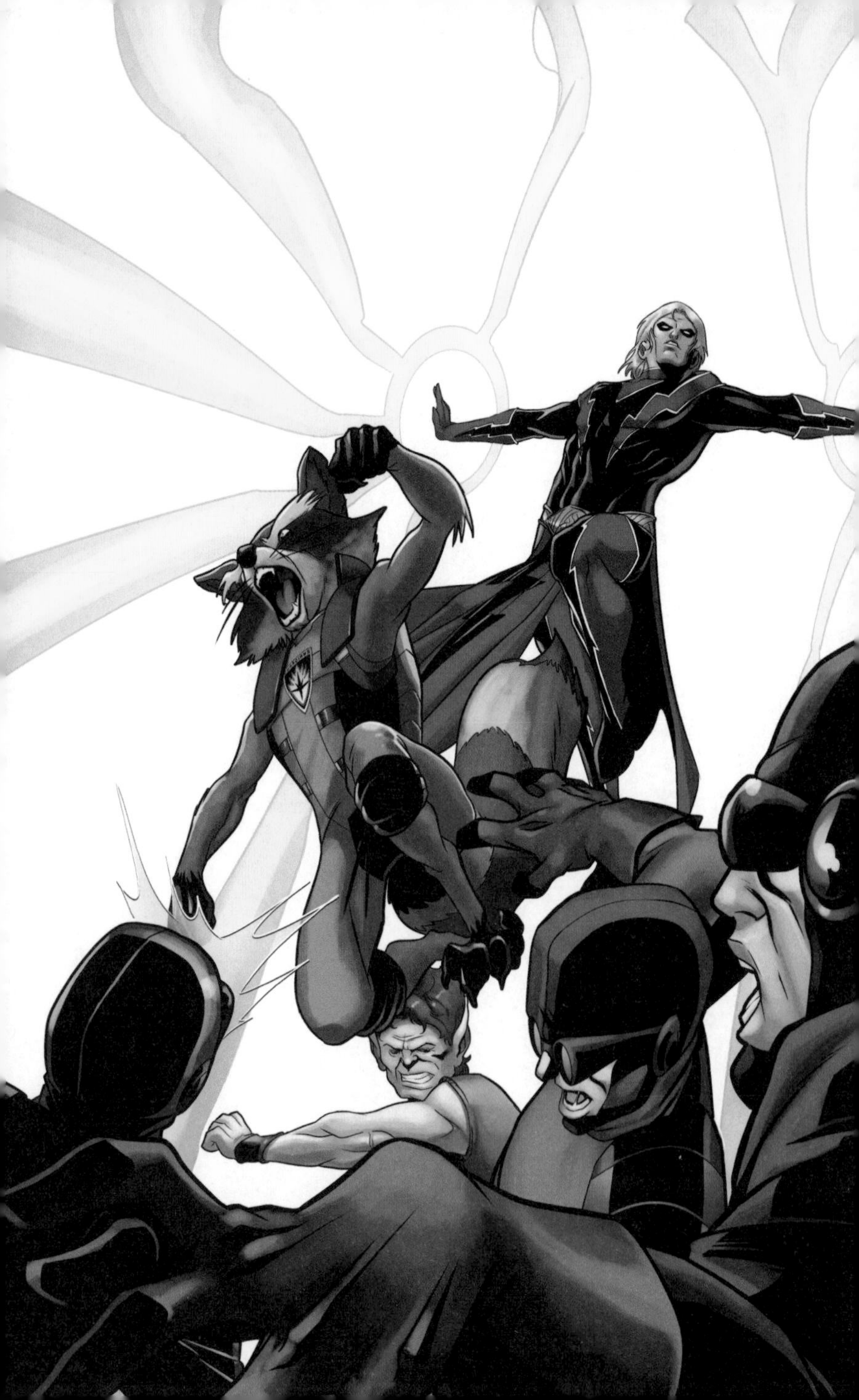

Gamora remembered exactly where she was. She wasn't really fighting her father—it was simply a dream, and she was in control. "This is not your story," she snarled, charging at Thanos and pushing him off the cliff. He made no sound as he fell, and for the first time in a very long while, Gamora felt a glimmer of peace.

Outside the cocoon, Rocket and Pip were taking fire from the Collector's minions.

"Hey, Warlock! How about you use some of that cosmic baloney and help us out here?" Rocket asked.

"My pleasure," Warlock said, moving into position. He used his cosmic energies to blast back the Collector's men as they struggled to gain ground.

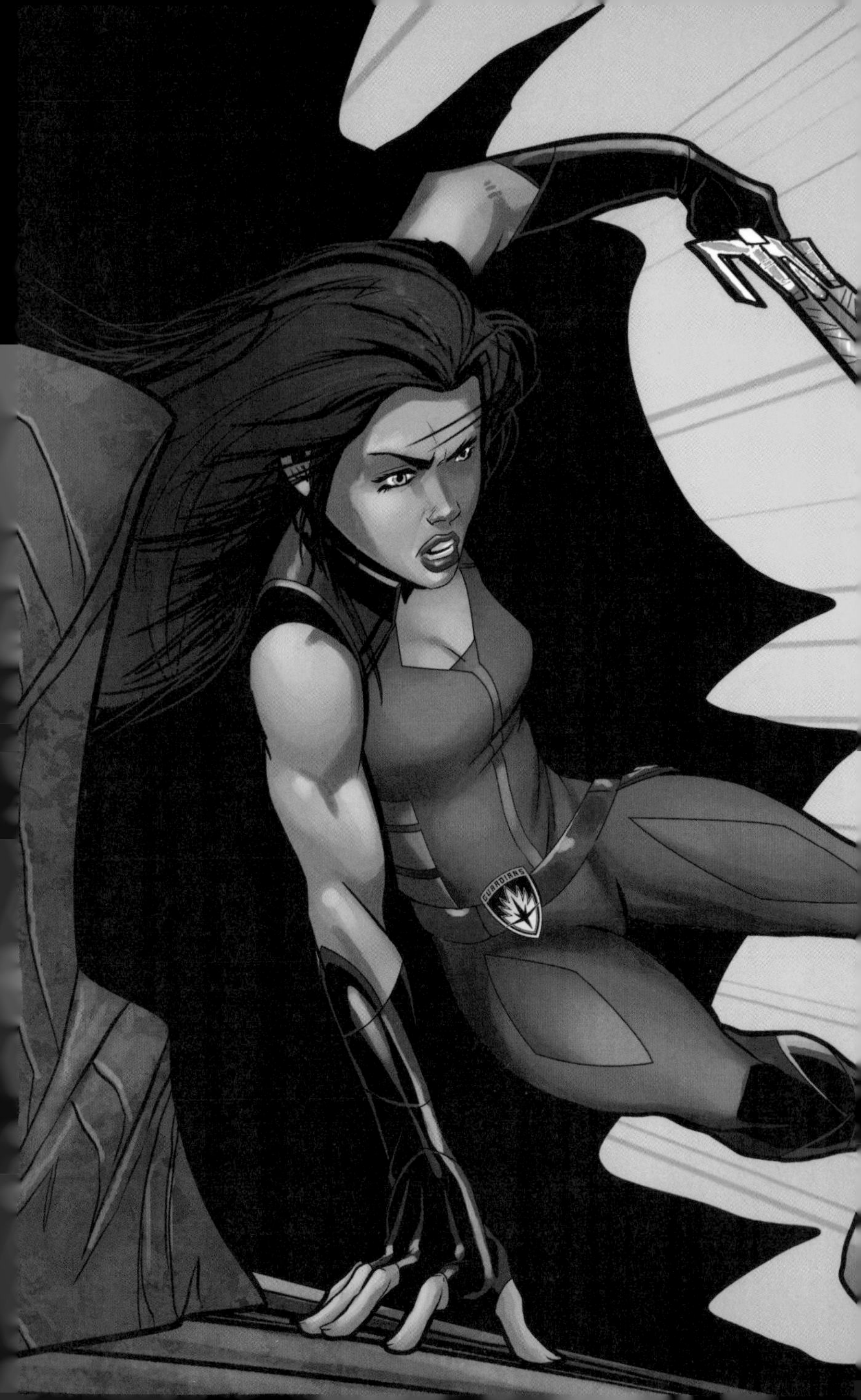
GUARDIANS

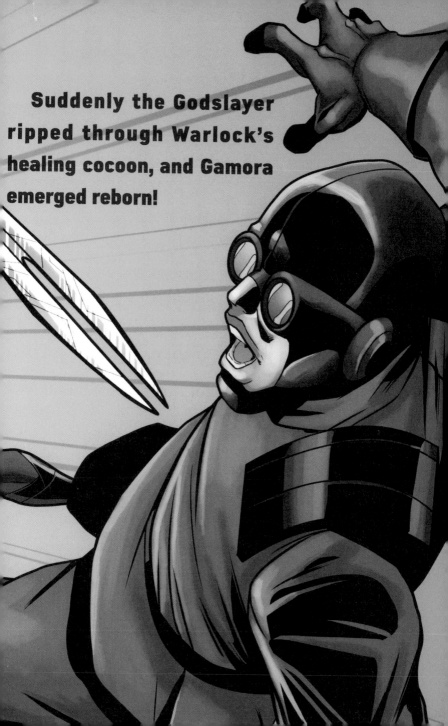

Suddenly the Godslayer ripped through Warlock's healing cocoon, and Gamora emerged reborn!

Gamora launched herself at the Collector's thugs with confidence and ease. She kicked their leader in the stomach, sending him flying out the door. Two more charged toward her, lasers firing. Gamora deflected their shots with the Godslayer and then sliced their plasma rifles in half. The largest goon aimed his weapon. He approached her slowly, growling like an animal. She scanned him, looking for his weakest points. As he inched closer, Gamora jumped into the air and pinched his neck, causing him to pass out cold. The remaining thugs retreated to their ship and took off. Rocket, Pip, and Adam Warlock came out from behind a large column, safe once again.

"So . . . how was your nap?" Rocket asked Gamora.

"Good," said Gamora, breathless. "I'm ready to leave this planet now."

Adam Warlock smiled. Gamora was back.

WATHOOM!!!

The ground shook as a new spacecraft landed outside the temple. It was Drax. He had received Pip's message before the ship lost power. Drax had tracked the signal and had come as quickly as he could.

"You rang?" Drax asked. **"I answered."**

CHAPTER 7

"It's time to go," Pip said, waving everyone toward Drax's ship.

Gamora was taking in the wonders of the ancient citadel before saying good-bye to Adam Warlock. "This temporary home of yours is truly amazing," she said, running her hand across the wall and feeling its intricate details. "There's so much history here."

"It's true. Many have come through this sanctuary over the years. Its history gives it definition," Warlock said. **"Does your history give you definition, Gamora?"**

Gamora paused to consider the question. Not anymore, she thought. Confronting and defeating her father in the dreamscape left Gamora feeling strong and empowered. The healing cocoon had done its job.

"Thank you, Adam. For your advice and for your friendship," Gamora said.

"We're all on a journey. I'm sure our paths will cross again very soon," Adam Warlock said.

"Good-bye, Warlock," added Drax. **"Till next time."**

Pip glanced up at Gamora, Adam Warlock, and Drax standing in formation. **"Look at us!"** he chuckled. **"The old crew back together again and kicking butt."**

"Emphasis on *OLD*," said Rocket. **"C'mon, troll! Stop blubbering about the past. Get in the ship and let's wrap up this adventure already."**

As the group settled into their voyage, Drax took a moment to catch up with Gamora. **"I've missed our sparring sessions,"** he confided. **"You're the only battler on this team that's been able to match me blow for blow."**

"HEY! I'm offended!" Rocket groused. **"I like to think I'm pretty good with my fists."**

"From what I've seen, you only use them to stuff your face with snacks," Pip said.

"Enough chatter," Drax said. **"Tell me where we're heading, troll."**

"I've tracked Nebula to a place called SAKAAR," Pip said, activating the ship's holographic projection. **"Sakaar is the fourth planet**

in the Tayo Star System, located in the Fornax Galaxy. If you like giant, nasty monsters, this place is for you. The creatures who live there are savage, and the terrain is hazardous. This won't be a vacation. Don't make the Drammoths angry, or you'll be in big trouble. We'll need to be ready for anything."

"No. You won't," said Gamora. "Because I'm going in alone."

"What?! That's crazy, and you know it," Rocket exclaimed. **"Didn't that freaking cocoon teach you anything?"**

"I must confront Nebula by myself. She'll do anything to watch me suffer, and that includes hurting my friends and the people I care for. I won't risk your lives for my own needs," Gamora explained. "I'm a warrior, and I will complete this task alone. End of story."

"A warrior can be hard

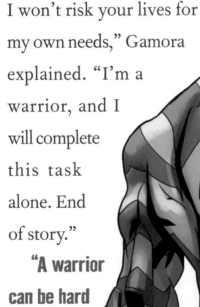

and soft at the same time. This is a lesson I have learned in my life that I will share with you now," said Drax, placing his hand on Gamora's shoulder. "I lost my family to violence. It gave me much pain. My emotions altered my mind, and I could not think straight. But then I found hope. It was with you and the Guardians. You are my family now." Drax powered down the ship's thrusters. "Gamora, you have my respect and admiration. But I will not take you to Sakaar unless we fight together as a family."

"Yeah. Me too," Rocket said. "You going in alone? It ain't right."

"I hate to admit it, but the hairy crybaby is right," Pip agreed. "We're in this together, kid. For better or for worse, you're stuck with us."

Gamora took in the moment and realized how lucky she truly was. No matter how alone she may have felt, her friends were there when she needed them. It was time to accept their help and get going. "Let's do this," she said, unsheathing her blade and moving it gently so it glinted in the light.

"I have a question," said Drax. "Why are we chasing Nebula?"

"It's all because of some mystery box," Pip answered.

"Hmmm. This all seems very familiar. Are you sure we have not done this before?" asked Drax.

"We're always chasing down mystery boxes, cosmic cubes, and Infinity Stones. That's just what we do. We're the Guardians of the Galaxy!"

Rocket said, glancing at Pip and frowning. "**And a troll. We're the Guardians of the Galaxy and a troll.**"

"**If it brings Gamora peace, I will do it. What is our plan?**" Drax inquired.

Gamora thoughtfully considered the question. "We're going to find Nebula, retrieve what belongs to me, and stomp any beasts that get in the way," she said. "How does that sound?"

"**Sounds like a good plan to me,**" Drax said, firing up the thrusters and rocketing the ship toward **Sakaar.**

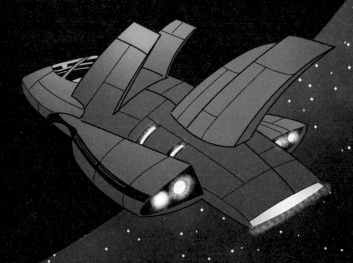

CHAPTER 8

"**Just once, I want to end up on a planet where no one is trying to kill me,**" Rocket said, polishing his plasma blaster. "**I don't think that's too much to ask.**"

The group touched down on **Sakaar** and prepared themselves for battle. Drax used his ship's computer to scan the area for danger.

"**This planet's terrain is treacherous and unpredictable. Be careful. Do not stray from the group,**" Drax explained as a variety of heinous

holograms appeared before
them: **the MawKaw
Magkong lava monster,
tentacled Amebids,** and

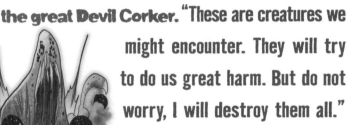

the great Devil Corker. "These are creatures we
might encounter. They will try
to do us great harm. But do not
worry, I will destroy them all."

"I appreciate that, Drax,"
Gamora said, turning
her attention to the group. "I know I
haven't said much on this journey,
but I want you all to know that your
friendship and camaraderie mean a
great deal to me. Whatever
happens out there, know
that all of you are—"

"**Don't sweat it, kid!**" Rocket interrupted. "**No need for mushy stuff. This is what we do. Now let's go kick some butt.**"

The ship's door opened as Drax, Rocket, Pip, and Gamora carefully stepped outside. The air was dry, the wind filled with sand. They'd landed in one of Sakaar's flat deserts, surrounded by mountains and gorges. In the distance sat Nebula's fortress, a medium-size cavelike structure. On the outside it seemed harmless enough, but getting there wouldn't be easy.

"So we walk from here to there? That's not dangerous at all! You guys are a bunch of babies," Pip said, striding proudly toward their objective. Suddenly, the ground below them shook violently. The surface of the planet cracked open, boulders flying in all directions as a gigantic Wildebot emerged from Sakaar's craggy depths. Wildebots were technology-based nonorganic life-forms from the planet **Cron** whose spaceship crash-landed on Sakaar after being pulled through the Great Portal. They weren't happy about the relocation. The beast scooped Pip up into his metal hand and scowled at the little troll as if he were a naughty pet.

Drax sighed. **"Pip, there is a reason we are no longer on the same team,"** he groused, launching himself onto the back of the steel beast. Drax pounded his fists into it over and over again like a jackhammer, pulverizing the creature's metal body into a million little pieces and ripping its circuitry apart until it was completely dismantled. Pip thanked his old friend, and they continued on their path. As they approached their destination, Nebula appeared.

"You're so predictable, Gamora. A troll, an animal, and a sad fighting creature? You've already lost," Nebula taunted.

"You underestimate my associates," announced Gamora.

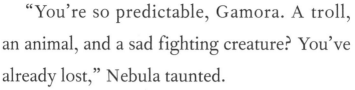

"**AND I AM NOT SAD!**" Drax shouted.

A gathering army of Chitauri soldiers appeared from inside Nebula's cavern compound. They were ready and waiting to serve her every evil need. "These were a gift from Thanos, to be used for protection, destruction, or whatever I desire. Today I will use them for everything," she said. "And our father will be so pleased when they end up defeating you."

"**Chitauri?!**" whined Rocket. "**Those guys are rubes!**"

"Thanos cares nothing for life," Gamora told her sister. "The welfare of others has no value or meaning to a despot like him. This is your role model? This is the person you seek to please? One day, when he's done using you, Thanos will cast you aside as he has done with everything else. I take no pleasure in what I do here today."

Nebula's body filled with red rage. **"ATTACK!"** she commanded as the battalion

of Chitauri warriors stormed toward Gamora and her allies. The heroes swiftly ducked for cover behind a group of nearby boulders. The Chitauri blasted them with fire as Nebula disappeared into her stronghold.

"I'm going after Nebula," Gamora said. **"Cover me!"** She took off toward her sister, deflecting lasers with her blade.

"MUNCH ON LASER, SKULL FACES!" Rocket said, blasting away at the incoming army. As the Chitauri descended upon them, Drax ran onto the battlefield, using his body as a battering ram, taking on soldiers left and right. Pip continued to hide.

FIZZZZZZZZUUUUUUU!

Rocket's plasma blaster powered down without warning. **"My gun!"** he exclaimed, tinkering with its settings. **"This is bad."**

Pip ran to Rocket's aid. "Let me have a look," Pip said, cracking open the weapon. "Here's your problem. Your secondary particle ionization chamber is stuck." He flipped a switch, and the blaster was back up and running.

"Hey, thanks, troll," Rocket said. **"You're not so bad. Still hairy, but not so bad. Now let's take these Chitauri flarknards down!"**

Safely away from the battle, Gamora cautiously entered Nebula's cavern fortress.

The inside seemed hollow and empty. It reminded her of her father.

"I'm done with these games, sister!" Gamora shouted. "The box belongs to me."

"You want this so badly," Nebula sneered, holding up the metal box. "And yet you know nothing of what is inside. It controls you."

"Nothing controls me. Not anymore," Gamora said, striking a defensive stance. "Hand over the box."

"You will open the box for me," Nebula said, pressing her hand against the wall and activating a control panel. The wall behind her parted to reveal a prison cell containing the unconscious bodies of **Star-Lord** and **Groot**.

"Or you will never see your friends again," Nebula declared.

CHAPTER 9

Nebula delighted in unveiling the captive Star-Lord and Groot. Gamora had been preparing herself to confront her sister for a long time. She saw it as her mission to end their conflict once and for all, but she never expected that two of her best friends' lives would hang in the balance. The two sisters were locked in a stare-down. Gamora's silence drove Nebula crazy, and she soon demanded a response.

"What will it be, sister?" Nebula taunted.

Drax, Rocket, and Pip raced into the fortress, out of breath and fresh from battle. They were shocked to see their teammates trapped in Nebula's clutches.

"**What the—?!**" muttered Rocket. "**Our friends got flarknarded!**"

"**Now I'm angry,**" Drax growled.

"**And I bet we wouldn't like you when you're angry, right? You know, like that other green guy, the incredible one?**" quipped Pip as the assembled group stared flatly. "**Sorry, bad joke. Just forget I ever said it.**"

"WHAT IS YOUR ANSWER, GAMORA?" Nebula shouted.

"I'll do it," Gamora solemnly replied. "I'll give you what you want."

"What?! Gamora, don't do this," Rocket said in a whispered plea. **"Don't give in! We'll find another way. Can't we give the troll to Nebula instead?"** Despite the great danger they faced, Gamora's allies always found comfort in humor.

"It's okay, Rocket," Gamora said in a pacifying tone. "It'll be all right." She gently made her way toward Nebula, relaxing her body with each step. It was pleasing to finally confront her sister face-to-face. Gamora glanced back at her allies and felt proud. She gave a slight nod to Drax, then turned her attention to the box.

"Open it," Nebula commanded. "Place your finger on the mark and open it."

Gamora looked her sister in the eyes and

grinned. Everything was going to be all right. In the blink of an eye, she snatched the box right out of Nebula's hands and, with a swift kick, knocked her sister off her feet. "Follow me if you dare," Gamora snarled, brandishing her Godslayer and taking off on foot across the wilds of Sakaar.

"RRAAHHHH!" Nebula screamed. She rose from the ground in anger,

brushed herself off, and scrambled to chase after Gamora. Rocket and Pip wanted to free Star-Lord and Groot, but there were two problems standing in front of them. Nebula left behind a duo of Chitauri soldiers to guard her prisoners, and they weren't budging. Pip had an idea.

"Distract these two, wouldja?" he whispered to Rocket. "I'm going to try something."

Rocket nodded and began dancing around like a fool, drawing attention to himself. **"YIYIYIYIYIYIYI! I'm a hairy little squirt, ain't I? Please don't hurt me, big scary bad guys!"** babbled Rocket as Pip secretly slipped behind the Chitauri. He grabbed them by the shoulders and, in a flash, the burly soldiers disappeared into thin air. **"What the what?!"** exclaimed Rocket. **"Did you just teleport those guys away?!"**

Pip grinned. "Huh. Guess my powers aren't as rusty as I thought they were! Now grab your pals,"  he said as Rocket rushed to free Star-Lord and Groot, who had just woken up. Both of them were groggy and confused; neither one knew where they were or how they'd gotten there.

"Whahaaaaaa? Where am I?" asked a dizzy Star-Lord. "We were heading to **Spartax**, and then there was a light, and now we're here?"

"I AM GROOT?" said a weary Groot, struggling to stay awake. Rocket began trying different combinations to unlock the cell, but nothing was working.

"My head hurts," said Star-Lord, pointing in the distance. "And there's a monster."

"Awww. The poor guy must still be dreaming," said Pip cheerfully.

"ROOOAAARRR!"

An enormous Drammoth had crawled into the chamber, licking its lips and eyeing Pip as if he were a tasty little morsel.

"Not dreaming!" said a frightened Pip.

Drax turned to confront the creature head-on. **"I hate Sakaar,"** he grumbled, charging the Drammoth with a fiery passion.

Across the desert of Sakaar, Gamora ran for

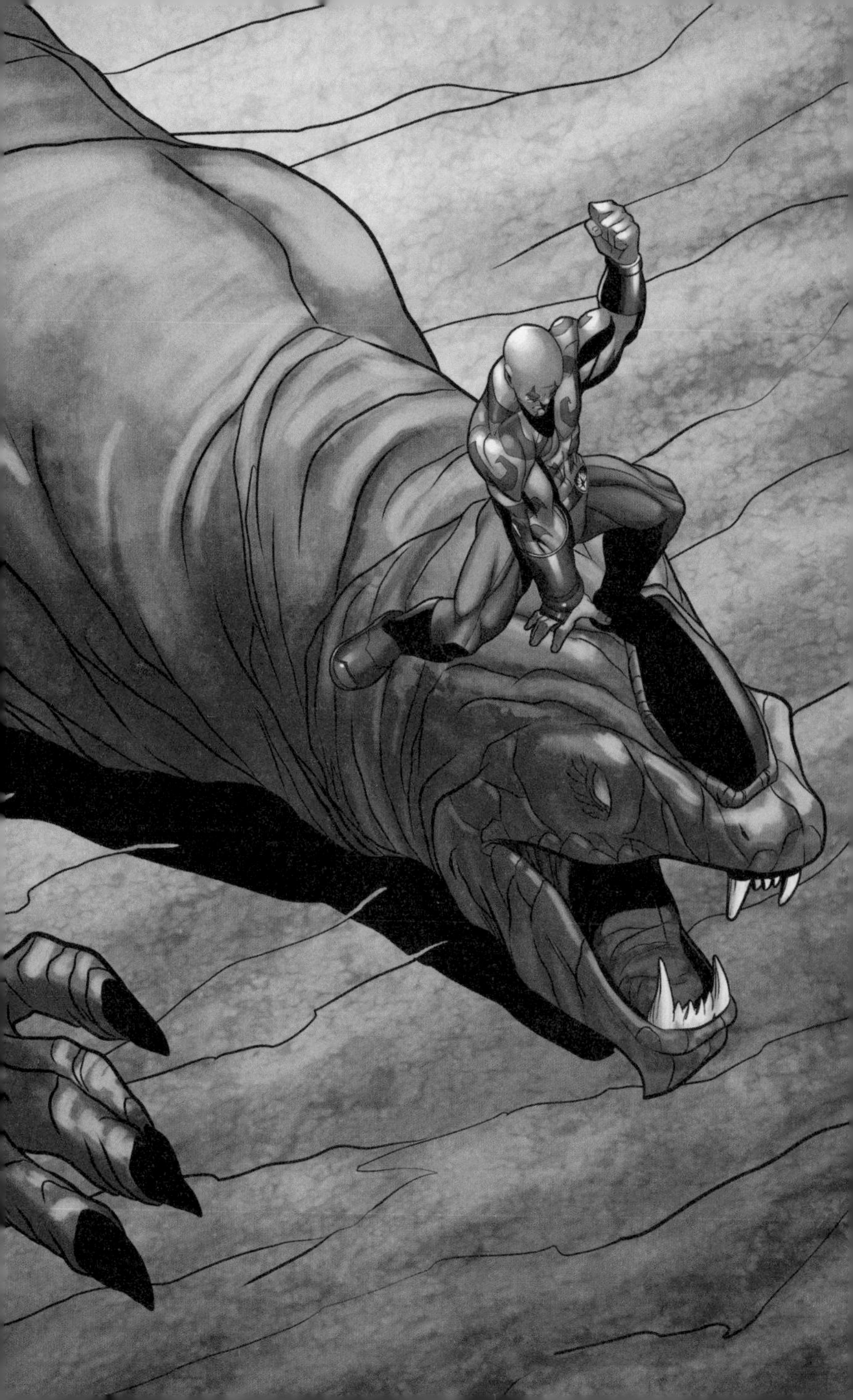

miles through the planet's empty wastelands. She clutched the mystery box tightly as Nebula gave chase. They'd been running for a while, their pace becoming slower as their energy depleted. Gasping for breath, they both stopped to rest at the edge of a deep gorge.

"Well? **OPEN IT!**" commanded Nebula. "You have what you want, now do what you came here to do!"

"I came here to offer my hand in peace, Nebula," confided Gamora. "We're family."

"LIAR!" Nebula screamed. "You only care for yourself. Thanos took us in. He gave us our lives, and you thank him by disobeying, by running away from your heritage! Family? Ha! You don't do that to family."

"Family doesn't hurt you," Gamora began.

"Family is about the people who have your back when the odds are stacked against you. I have a family—and they are the Guardians of the Galaxy. I didn't come here to fight you, but I will." Gamora tucked the box into the back of her belt and made sure her sword was tightly secured. If she was going to battle her sister,

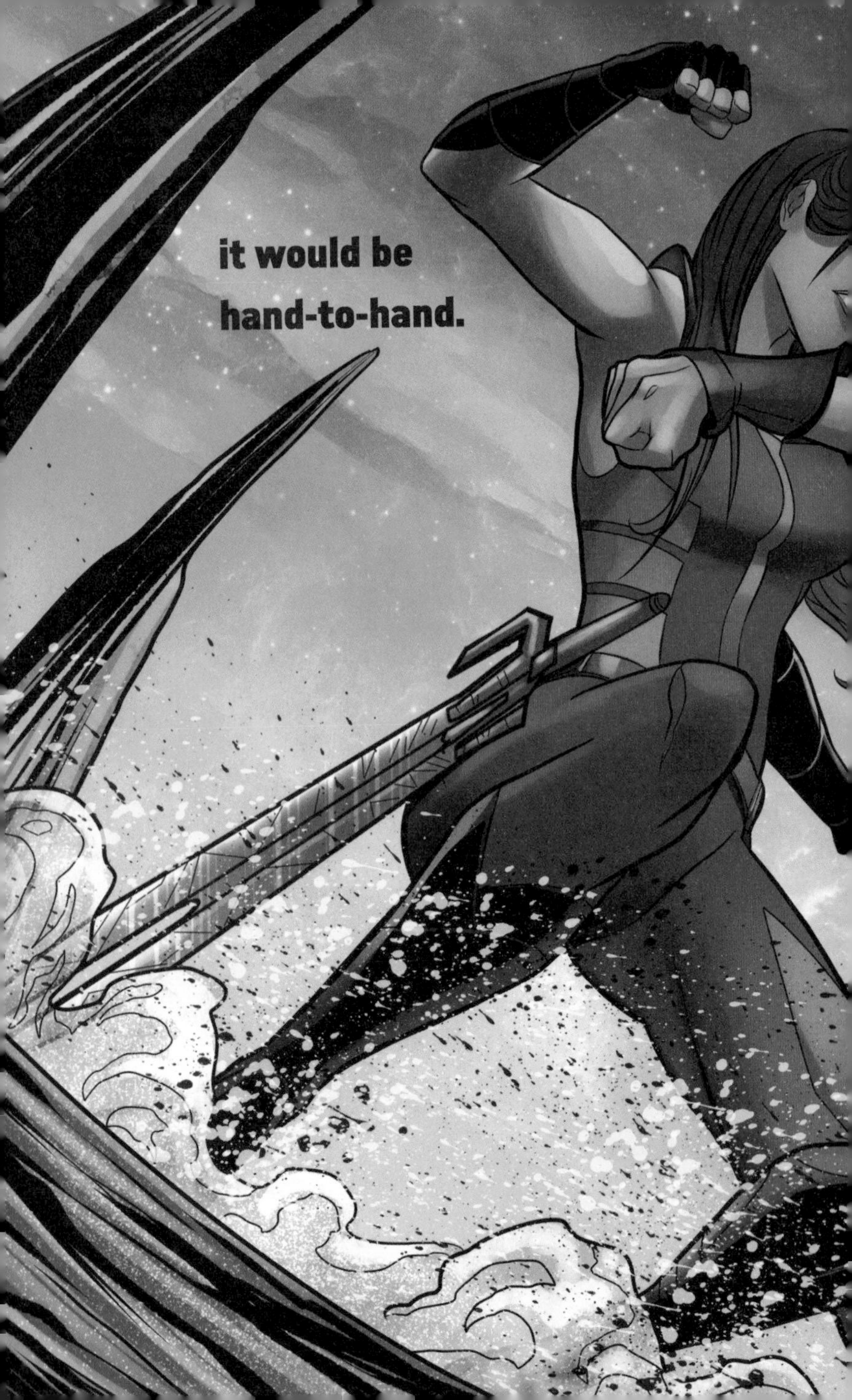
it would be
hand-to-hand.

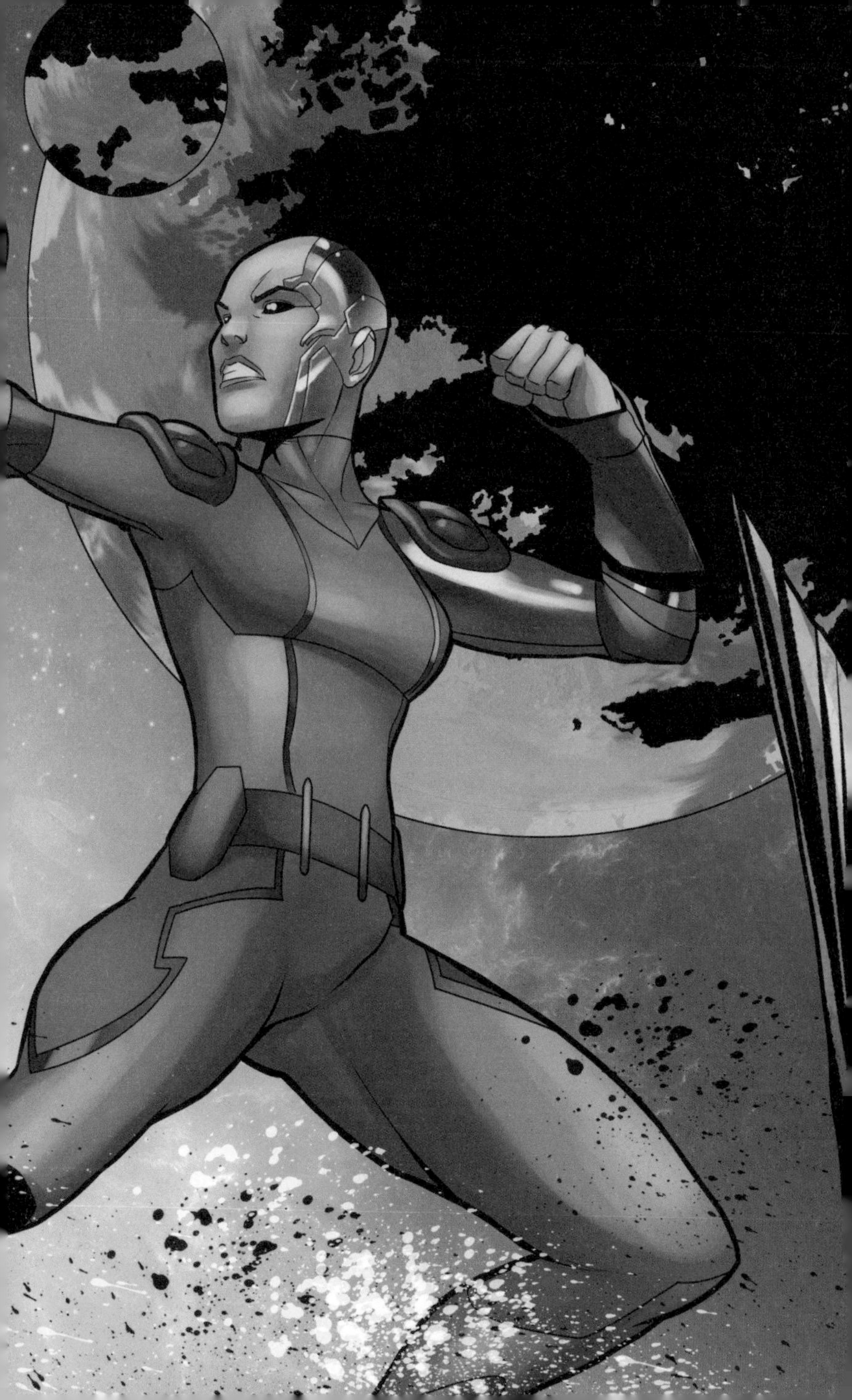

Nebula flung herself, hands outstretched, toward Gamora. But Gamora ducked to avoid her sister's grasp, whipping around to grab Nebula's arm and hold it firmly behind her back. Nebula used all of her strength to flip Gamora over her own body. Nebula raised her leg to stomp her sister into the ground, but Gamora caught her foot and tossed her back hastily. Gamora flung herself up, jumping on top of Nebula and pinning her to the ground. They were growing tired.

"Mercy, sister," Nebula pleaded. Gamora loosened her grip slightly. Nebula used it to her advantage, grabbing Gamora by the arm and hurling her to the ground. "Fool."

Gamora lay there in silence. "Maybe I am a fool for believing you'd ask for mercy," she said. "But that's the difference between us. When someone asks for help, I give it."

"It wasn't always like this, Gamora," Nebula said. "Do you remember when we were little girls, battling one another for Father's affection?"

"We didn't know any better," Gamora said, picking herself up and dusting off her shoulders. "But now we do, and it's time to move on!"

CREEEEEECH!

A monstrous Devil Corker burst from the ground, snatching up Nebula with its spiked tongue and tossing her from side to side. Devil Corkers were terrifying creatures, native to the Upper Vandro region of Sakaar. Beastly-looking arachnids, they had a habit of lurking below-ground, waiting for their prey. This particular creature felt movement and swiftly went in for the kill. There was no time for Gamora to think.

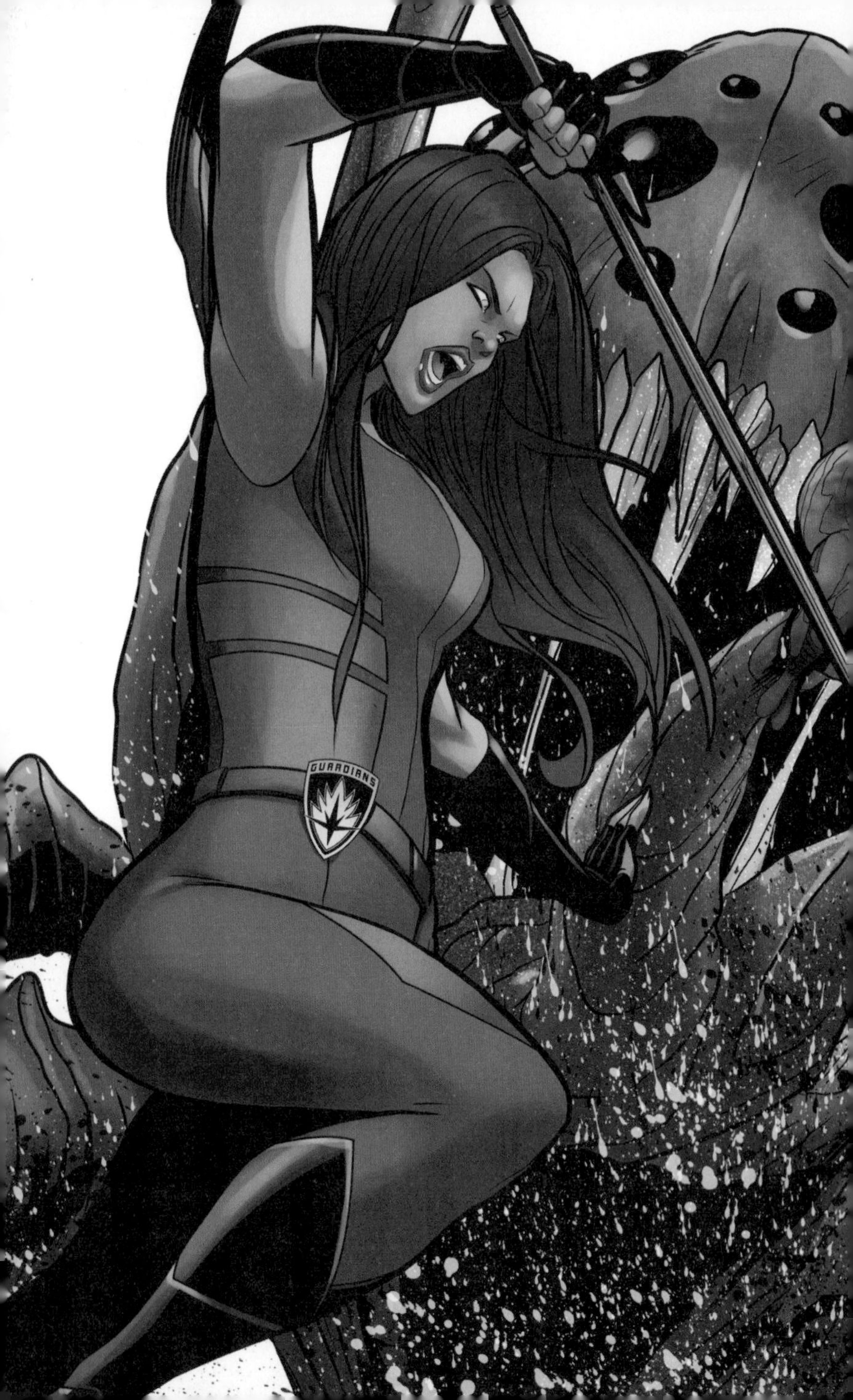
GUARDIANS

She leaped onto the monster's enormous head. Then she pulled her blade from its sheath and punctured the creature, causing it to drop Nebula and cry out in pain. Gamora used her remaining strength to thrust the beast down into the nearby gorge before jumping to safety.

The duo lay there on the ground in silence, drained by the unrelenting struggle. They had been through so much together—both as sisters and warriors—but the wounds of the past weren't healing. Perhaps, one day, that would change. Gamora wondered whether today was that day.

SHZZZAK!

Gamora sat up in an instant. Nebula had vanished, using her wrist gauntlets to teleport away. She'll be back, Gamora thought, but I got the box. Although she was spent physically, Gamora smiled—she was happy. Change was in the air.

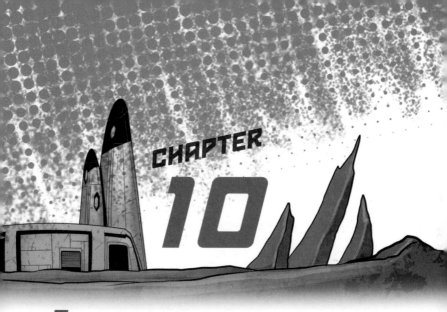

CHAPTER 10

*T*he trek back to Nebula's base was long but worth it. It gave Gamora time to think. She'd retrieved what she came for—and, though her sister escaped, she believed Nebula may have been changed for the better. Only time will tell, she thought. Rocket, Drax, and Pip were more than happy to see that she'd returned mostly unscathed.

"You got the box! Nice job. Can we leave now?" Rocket said wearily. **"Hey, where's Nebby, anyway?"**

"She teleported off the planet," explained

Gamora. "She'll appear again, somewhere, someday, and we'll be ready for her."

"Can someone please explain what's happening?!" Star-Lord pleaded.

"Do not worry about it, Quill," assured Drax. "Just be quiet."

"I AM GROOT!" demanded Groot.

"Don't worry, buddy. We'll definitely get you home," Rocket assured his friend. "We're all going home, right?" He looked deep into Gamora's eyes, wondering whether she'd end her vacation and rejoin the team. From the looks of it, he wasn't about to take no for an answer.

"There is no place I'd rather be than with my tribe," Gamora replied.

"This is good news," Drax said. "Now, everyone get in the ship so we can leave this

place behind." A Drammoth's roar rang out in the distance. **"I hate Sakaar."**

"Where is home for you guys?" asked Pip.

"THE GALAXY," scoffed Rocket. **"Duh."**

The group piled into the spacecraft and left Sakaar for good. As they soared high into the sky, Rocket pawed at the mystery box, desperate to see what was inside.

"OooOooOoo! I hope it's an Infinity Stone. Or maybe it's money! We could use some of that. We could also use some troll deodorant," said Rocket, wincing. **"I can barely breathe in here."**

"Leave it alone," Pip piped in. "It's Gamora's thing, let her do what she wants with it."

TRoLL DeoDoRANT

"**You know what? The troll is right,**" Rocket concluded. "**I don't care what's inside of it anymore. As long as Gamora is happy, so am I.**"

"**WHAT IS GOING ON?!**" yelped Star-Lord.

"We'll explain everything," Gamora assured him. "Someday."

"Hey, can you drop me off on Degenera?" asked Pip.

"**Oh, no. No way am I going back to that stinkin' hole,**" Rocket said, scrunching his nose. "**They stole my ship! What am I going to tell the rental company? That place is bad news.**"

"Then I guess I'll just stay with you guys and become a Guardian of the Galaxy," joked Pip. "We can hang out forever and ever and ever and—"

"**TO DEGENERA!**" shouted Rocket.

"No," said Gamora. "To **Zaldrex**. We have work to do."

Rocket remembered the ugliness they'd witnessed at the thieves' market. **"Oh, yeah! That's right. We do have some work to do. TO ZALDREX!"**

"And call **Captain Marvel**," Gamora suggested. "We're going to need all of the help we can get."

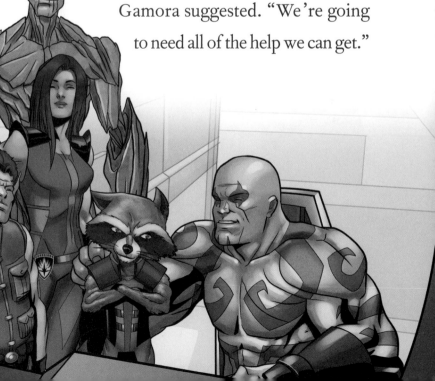

Gamora strolled to the back of the ship by herself. It felt good to be surrounded by her teammates once again, but she needed a moment alone. She gingerly studied the box that had given her so much hope and heartache. It felt lighter than she remembered. Was it a tyrant's trinket, or was it something else? The question no longer mattered. Gamora pulled a tiny explosive device from her pocket. She stuck the small blinking gadget to the box, placed it inside the air lock,

and closed the shuttle door tightly. Taking a deep breath, she opened the air lock, and the box was sucked out into the void of space. In a matter of moments, a blinding burst of light flashed before Gamora's eyes. The box had been destroyed. Her quest was finally over. A weight lifted from her shoulders. She realized that once she'd retrieved the box, its contents didn't really matter. She'd lived without knowing for a long time, and now revealing what was inside no longer felt important. What the box represented was the burden of her past. Now, at last, she was free. It was time to move forward. As the ship moved through the cosmos, a sun's bright rays shone through the window, warming Gamora's face. A new day was dawning, and she was spending it with her family.

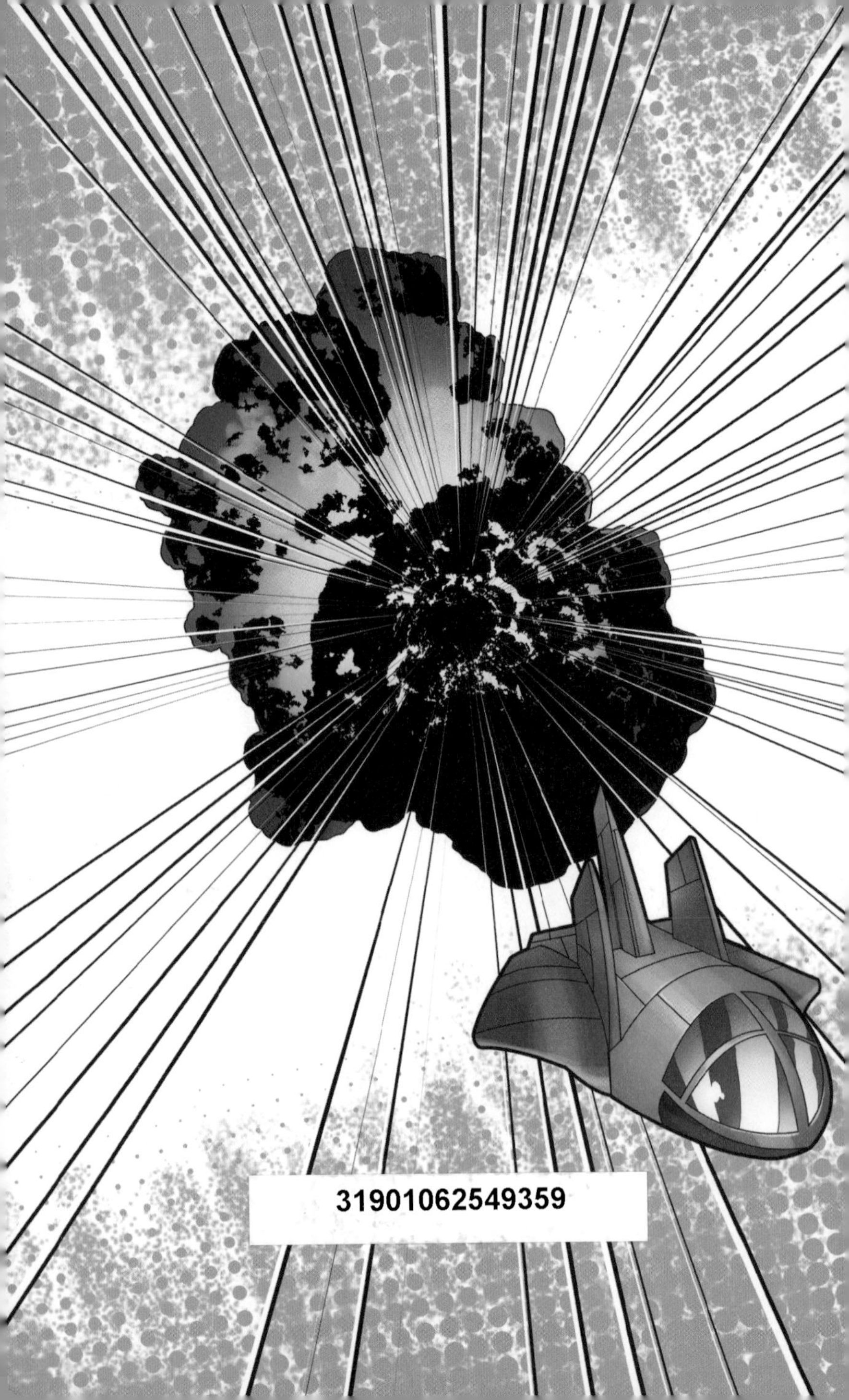